Little Pickle and Greedy Giant

Written by Helen Dineen

Illustrated by Elif Balta Parks

Collins

Greedy Giant was sitting at the table. Her stomach rumbled loudly.

She nibbled a carrot. "These vegetables taste terrible!" she said.

She pushed the plate away.

Little Pickle scrambled up and carefully poked the tiny vegetables, which didn't look very tasty.

"Can you show me your garden?" he asked.
"Of course," replied Greedy Giant.

Little Pickle soon saw the problem.

"I would be happy to help you look after the garden,"
he told the giant. "We can grow tasty vegetables here."

"The vegetable patch is covered in weeds. Let's tackle them," said Little Pickle.

Greedy Giant shouted "Charge!" and rushed into the dense jungle.

"Gently!" said Little Pickle. They quickly filled a wheelbarrow.

"These tomatoes need plenty of sunlight to help them grow," said Little Pickle.

He helped Greedy Giant put up a large greenhouse for the tomatoes.

"Gently!" said Little Pickle.

"The earth is extremely dry," said Little Pickle.
"It needs water. Let's give the thirsty vegetables
a drink."

Suddenly, Greedy Giant jumped. Little Pickle yelled, "What is it?"

"That beetle startled me!" whimpered Greedy Giant.
"Don't be scared," said Little Pickle.

The little beetle scuttled across Greedy Giant's hand.
Greedy Giant was very gentle.

Slowly, the vegetable patch grew. Little Pickle looked after the vegetables well.

Greedy Giant pulled up horrible weeds and carefully rescued creepy crawlies. Until one day ...

Greedy Giant saw that all the vegetables were giant too! What an impressive vegetable patch!

Greedy Giant carried some gigantic red tomatoes.
Little Pickle struggled with a huge bundle of carrots!

Little Pickle and Greedy Giant tucked in. "These are the most incredible vegetables I have ever eaten," said Greedy Giant.

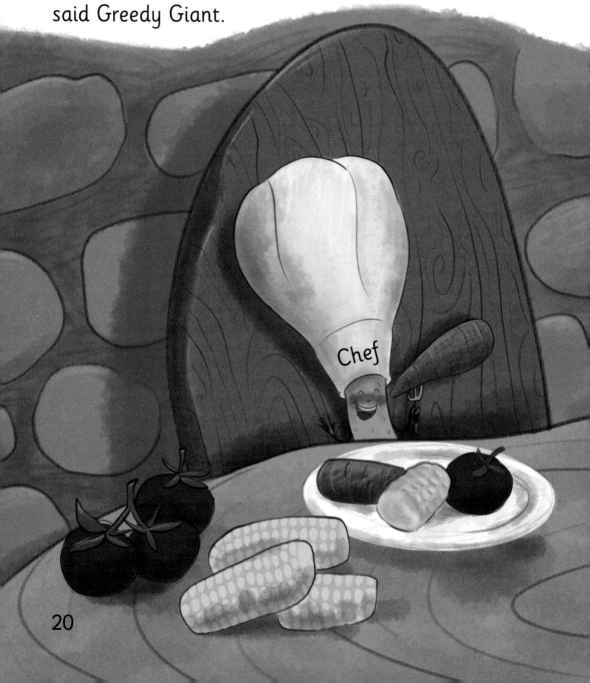

They greedily gobbled the lot. What a feast!

Greedy Giant's garden

After reading

Letters and Sounds: Phase 5

Word count: 288

Focus phonemes: /ai/ a /ee/ e-e, e, y /oo/ u /igh/ ie, y /ch/ tch /sh/ ch /c/ ch /j/ g, ge /l/ le /w/ wh /v/ ve /s/ se

Common exception words: of, to, the, into, are, said, one, water, friend, were

Curriculum links: Science: Plants

National Curriculum learning objectives: Reading/word reading: apply phonic knowledge and skills as the route to decode words, read other words of more than one syllable that contain taught GPCs; Reading/comprehension: drawing on what they already know or on background information and vocabulary provided by the teacher

Developing fluency

- Your child may enjoy hearing you read the book.
- Take turns to read the main text. Check that your child notices the ellipsis on page 17; if necessary demonstrate how pausing at the ellipsis adds suspense.

Phonic practice

- Turn to pages 4 and 5. Challenge your child to find as many different spellings of the /ee/ sound as possible:

  y – *carefully, tiny, very, tasty, Greedy*

  e – *me, he*

  ee – *Greedy*

- Turn to pages 8 and 9. How many words containing the /j/ sound can they find. (*vegetable, Giant, charge, jungle, gently*)

Extending vocabulary

- Ask your child to say how they would spell the ending of these words if they added -ly on the end:

  loud (*loudly*)   large (*largely*)

  careful (*carefully*)   extreme (*extremely*)

- Take turns to think of a word ending in the /ee/ sound, for the other to attempt to spell. (e.g. *tasty, plenty, lovely*)